ALLIGATORS
ALL AROUND

AN ALPHABET

ALLIGATORS ALL AROUND

by
MAURICE SENDAK

AN ALPHABET

SCHOLASTIC INC.
New York Toronto London Auckland Sydney

ISBN 0-590-45451-X

Copyright © 1962 by Maurice Sendak.
All rights reserved. Published by Scholastic Inc.,
730 Broadway, New York, NY 10003, by arrangement
with HarperCollins, Publishers.

30 29 28 27 26 25 24 23 22 21   0 1 2/0

Printed in the U.S.A.   08

First Scholastic printing, January 1992

 alligators all around

B

bursting balloons

C catching colds

D doing dishes

E entertaining elephants

F forever fooling

G getting giggles

H

having headaches

I imitating Indians

J juggling jelly beans

K keeping kangaroos

L

looking like lions

M
making macaroni

 never napping

O ordering oatmeal

P pushing people

quite quarrelsome

R riding reindeer

S shockingly spoiled

T throwing tantrums

U usually upside down

V very vain

W

wearing wigs

X x-ing x's

Y

yackety-yacking

Z

Zippity zound!
Alligators ALL around